THE LEGO MOVIE

unikitty

A Cuckoo Adventure

Written by
Samantha Brooke

SCHOLASTIC INC.

ISBN 978-0-545-79541-8

10 9 8 7 6 5 4 3 2 1   14 15 16 17 18 19/0

Based on the Screenplay by PHIL LORD & CHRISTOPHER MILLER
Based on the Story by DAN HAGEMAN & KEVIN HAGEMAN and PHIL LORD & CHRISTOPHER MILLER
Special thanks to Katrine Talks and Matthew Ashton.

Printed in the U.S.A.   40

First printing, September 2014

Hiyee! I am Princess UniKitty, and I welcome you all to Cloud Cuckoo Land!

This is my home, which is hidden way up in the sky, at the top of a rainbow among marshmallowy white clouds.

I'm going to tell you the story of the most exciting day ever: the day the Special came to Cloud Cuckoo Land!

You see, Cloud Cuckoo Land is the home of many Master Builders. Master Builders are super-creative people (like me!) who can build anything out of anything. And the Special was coming to meet them.

According to a prophecy, the Special was the person who could find the long-lost Piece of Resistance. This piece was the one and only thing that could stop Lord Business from taking over the world.

We have a saying in Cloud Cuckoo Land: "Any idea is a good idea except the not-happy ones." And Lord Business definitely did *not* have happy ideas.

He wanted everything his way, and for things to stay the same permanently. His plan was to glue the whole world together with a super weapon called the Kragle.

But a world without creativity would be like a bubble bath without bubbles. Boring.

Three Master Builders named Wyldstyle, Batman, and Vitruvius brought the Special to Cloud Cuckoo Land. The Special's name was Emmet.

They had just escaped from Lord Business's evil robots who were trying to capture Emmet. If Emmet put the Piece of Resistance on the Kragle, he could stop Lord Business's plan.

I couldn't wait to show Emmet and his friends around! I took them up the twirly staircase, past cartwheeling clowns and dancing duckies. We were on our way to my puppy-shaped palace: the Dog.

Emmet looked as though his brain was going to pop like a party balloon. "Uh . . . I have no idea what's going on. Or what this place is . . . at all," he said.

I explained, "Here in Cloud Cuckoo Land there are no rules. There's no government, no bedtimes, no baby-sitters, no frowny faces, and no negativity of any kind."

"You just said the word *no*, like, a thousand times," said Wyldstyle.

"And there's also NO consistency!" I added. "After all, any idea is a good idea except the not-happy ones. Those you push deep inside where no one will ever, ever, EVER find them!"

Just then, a few not-so-happy thoughts popped into my head. They made my voice shake, and my horn got all itchy!

Uh-oh. That was not a good sign. I took a few deep breaths . . . three, two, one . . . there. I was happy again.

Vitruvius asked Emmet to make a speech to all the Master Builders. Emmet was so nervous. He hadn't made many speeches before, and he kind of messed it up. If Emmet didn't believe in himself, how could the Master Builders believe in him?

My horn started to get itchy again. But I thought about puppies sliding down a rainbow. *Whew.* All better.

Just then, Bad Cop burst in! He and his robots began blasting Cloud Cuckoo Land. They captured all of my Master Builder friends and put them in prison ships. I had never seen anything so horrible!

"We have to get Emmet out of here!" Wyldstyle cried.

We decided to build a submarine and escape underwater. Bad Cop's robots wouldn't follow us there.

Everyone got to work! I used my two favorite colors to build my parts: sour apple and watermelon. I built a paddling teddy bear for the front and a rainbow tail for the back.

Emmet seemed very confused.

"Don't worry about what the others are doing," said Vitruvius. "Embrace what is special about you."

It didn't take long before we finished the submarine and dove underwater.

Through the window, I could see Cloud Cuckoo Land crumbling and sinking to the ocean floor. "My home, it's gone."

I felt a feeling that I had never felt before. It was like the opposite of happiness. "I must stay positive. Deep breaths in and out. Bubble gum . . . butterflies . . . cotton candy . . ."

Emmet saw how upset I was and offered me a seat.

"What is *that*?" Batman asked.

"It's a Double-Decker Couch. I built it," Emmet said.

We all stared at him.

"Well, it seemed like a good idea at the time," Emmet said sheepishly. "But now I realize that it's not super helpful. I mean, you all just seem to know how to build such cool things."

Batman groaned. "You are so disappointing on so many levels."

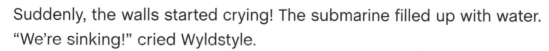

Suddenly, the walls started crying! The submarine filled up with water.
"We're sinking!" cried Wyldstyle.

The submarine broke apart, and the only thing that held together was
Emmet's couch. So we all hopped on and floated to safety.

Soon we were rescued by Metal Beard, another Master Builder.

"We need a new plan. And since Emmet's couch wasn't totally pointless, maybe he should come up with it," said Wyldstyle.

I nodded. Wyldstyle might seem like a hard candy on the outside, but I had a feeling she had a soft center inside for Emmet.

"Okay. . . " said Emmet. "Well, what's the last thing Lord Business would expect Master Builders to do?"

"Marry a marshmallow?" I suggested.

"No," said Emmet. "Follow the instructions!"

Emmet explained how we could build an ordinary-looking spaceship to sneak into Lord Business's super-tall tower. Then we could use the Piece of Resistance to stop the Kragle from gluing the world together.

We followed Emmet's instructions to build the ship. It looked so . . . boring.

I decided to pretty it up by adding flowers. But Emmet shook his head and reminded me that we had to follow the instructions. *Boo.*

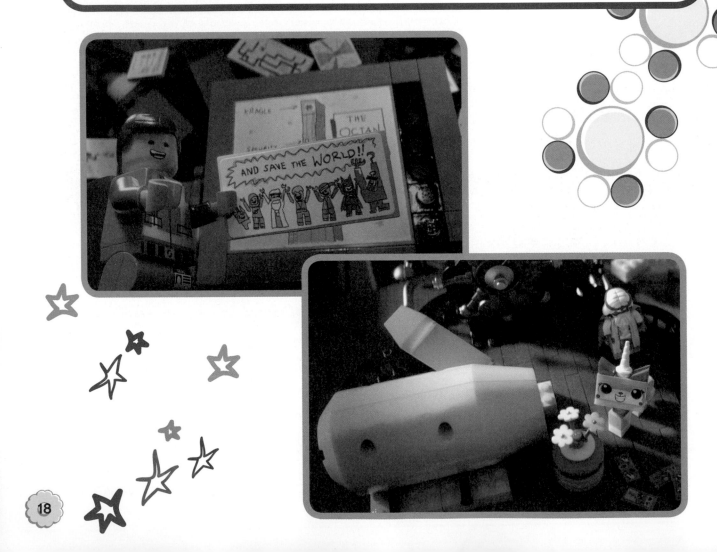

Emmet's plan worked! We got inside Lord Business's tower.

It was my job to distract Lord Business. So I disguised myself as a super-smart business executive. Batman helped, too. He was dressed as Bruce Wayne. Lord Business was really, *really* impressed by him.

Well, I could be impressive, too! "Business, business, business!" I cried. "Numbers. Money!"

I don't know what happened, but suddenly everything went wrong! Lord Business flew off in his Kraglizer to glue the whole world together!

That's when the most incredible, extra-awesome thing ever happened. Emmet finally believed in his specialness, and he built the most terrific robot suit.

"Go, Emmet!" I cheered as he charged toward Lord Business.

Instantly, Lord Business's robots flew to attack Emmet. That was *not* nice at all. "Must stay positive," I thought. I took a few deep breaths, but it didn't take me to my usual happy place. I couldn't stand seeing the robots trying to hurt my new friend, Emmet!

My horn went from itching to burning. It burned so hot that I turned completely red!

"YOU ALL NEED TO BE MORE FRIENDLY!" I screamed as I finally let out every last drippy drop of my anger. I leaped into the air and attacked all those mean robots.

"GO, EMMET, GO!" I yelled to Emmet as I cleared the path for him to get to Lord Business's Kraglizer. "You can do it!"

When Emmet reached the Kraglizer, he told Lord Business that he didn't want to fight. Lord Business was totally confused.

Instead, Emmet said, "You are the Special. And so am I. And so is everyone. You don't have to be a bad guy. You can still change everything."

No one had ever said anything like that to Lord Business. He thought for a moment . . . then he took the Piece of Resistance from Emmet and stopped the Kragle!

Emmet had changed so much since I'd first met him in Cloud Cuckoo Land. He'd dug deep down and found the most special parts of himself—the parts that were strong and creative.

And I had changed a little, too. But best of all, the Master Builders were free and everyone was able to be creative again. That meant the whole world had changed!

And that was the happiest thought of all.